If I Were an Animal!

by Woody

The Millbrook Press
Brookfield, Connecticut

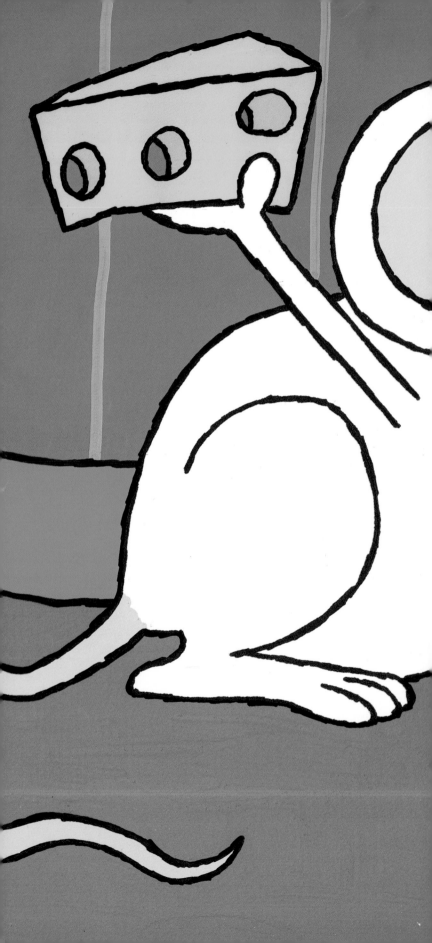

a white
mouse!

If I were an animal,
I would like to be ...

a spotty horse!

If I were an animal,
I would like to be ...

If I were an animal,
I would like to be ...

If I were
an animal,
I would like
to be ...

What animal would you like to be?